Wally Walrus

Barbara deRubertis
Illustrated by Jan Pyk

The Kane Press
New York

Cover Design: Sheryl Kagen

Library of Congress Cataloging-in-Publication Data

DeRubertis, Barbara.
Wally Walrus/Barbara deRubertis; illustrated by Jan Pyk.
p. cm.
"A let's read together book."--Cover.

Summary: Bad experiences with a bully make Wally the Walrus balk at going to school before he learns to call upon his natural abilities to prove himself.
ISBN 1-57565-046-0 (pbk. : alk. paper)
[1. Walruses--Fiction. 2. Bullies--Fiction. 3. Zoology--Polar regions--Fiction 4. Stories in rhyme.]
I. Pyk, Jan, 1934- ill. II. Title.
PZ8.3.D455Wal 1998
[E]--dc21   97-44315
                                                          CIP
                                                          AC

10 9 8 7 6 5 4 3

First published in the United States of America in 1998 by The Kane Press.
Printed in Hong Kong.

LET'S READ TOGETHER is a registered trademark of The Kane Press.

Wally Walrus
blinks and yawns.
The sky is pink.
A new day dawns.

Papa Walrus
calls to Wally.
"Rise and shine!"
His call is jolly.

3

Wally sprawls
across the bed.
He says, "I cannot
lift my head.

"I cannot go
to school today.
I will not go.
No school. No way."

Papa Walrus
asks, "Why not?
You've always liked
your school a lot!"

5

Wally draws
the covers up.
"Because . . .," he says.
"Sniff. Sniff. Hiccup."

Then Wally Walrus
starts to bawl.
"I don't like Squawky
Hawk at ALL.

"He bullies me with
squawks and caws.
He tries to scare me
with his claws.

"He says I'm slow as
slow can be.
He's always making
fun of me!"

7

Papa says,
"Let's take a walk.
I think we need
to have a talk."

Papa hauls
poor Wally out.
"Go brush your tusks.
And comb your snout."

9

Soon the pair
are on their walk.
They talk about
the naughty hawk.

Papa asks,
"What does he want?
Why does he like
to tease and taunt?"

Wally pauses.
"I know why.
When Squawky bullies
me, I cry.

"And when I cry,
he thinks he 'wins.'
He feels so BIG.
He smirks and grins."

Papa says,
"Don't LET him win.
Don't cry. And don't
act scared of him."

As Wally waddles
off to school,
he knows what he
must do. He's cool.

He watches for
that awful hawk.
Too soon he hears
that awful squawk.

Squawky screeches.
Squawky caws.
He reaches out with
hawky claws.

Naughty Squawky
flaps his wings.
"Slow-poke! Slow-poke!"
Squawky sings.

Wally Walrus
says, "Good-BYE.
You can't scare me
or make me cry."

He hauls himself
across the snow.
He's awkward, but
he is not slow!

Oh no! He slips!
Then Wally falls.

The ice is slick.
He spins! He sprawls!

18

He sees a caution
sign: "Beware!
Steep hill ahead!
Slow down! Take care!"

But Wally Walrus
cannot halt.
He can't slow down.
It's not his fault.

19

So Wally crouches
on his haunches.
Like a rocket
ship, he launches!

Wally vaults
into the air.
He somersaults
with grace and flair!

Then Wally dives
into the sea.
It is an awesome
thing to see!

Squawky can't
believe his eyes.
He drops his jaw.
What a surprise!

Wally swims
back to the shore.
And Squawky Hawk
applauds! "Do more!

"Do that again.
Please, Wally, do!
But this time, may
I ride with you?"

Wally's calm.
He slowly speaks.
"You've called me 'slow-
poke' now for weeks.

"Why would you want
to ride with me?
For I'm as *slow*
as slow can be!"

Squawky swallows,
drops his eyes,
and says, "I do
apologize.

"I've been a bully
and a brat.
I promise I will
stop all that."

27

So Wally takes
him for a ride.
They rocket down
the icy slide.

Squawky Hawk shouts
"Yippee-OH!"
It's like an Arctic
rodeo!

Their friends applaud.
They're cheering now . . .

as Wally Walrus
takes a bow!

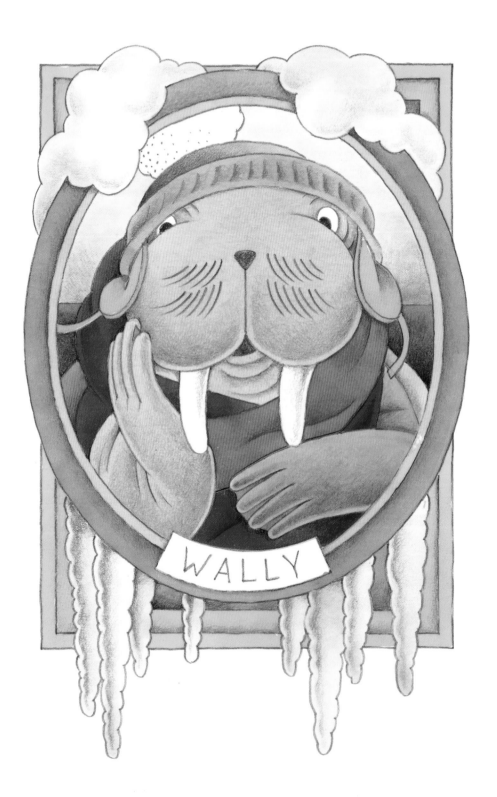

WALLY